THE AMAZING ADVENTURES OF NED NEDDINGTON

THE AMAZING ADVENTURES OF NED NEDDINGTON

BY
PAUL WEATHINGTON
with illustrations by Steve Shaw

JuneKat Books
Atlanta, Georgia

Published by
JuneKat Books, LLC
191 Peachtree Street NE, Suite 3900
Atlanta, Georgia 30303

ISBN 978-0-578-00923-0

Library of Congress Control Number: 2009921621

Printed in Canada by Friesens Corporation

Jacket and book design by Burtch Hunter Design

Contact Information

For ordering information, upcoming books
and information on our company, please visit us on the web at:

www.JuneKatBooks.com

Or contact us by mail at:

JuneKat Books, LLC
191 Peachtree Street NE, Suite 3900
Atlanta, Georgia 30303
Telephone: 404-524-1600 • Fax: 404-524-1610

CONTENTS

To all seven of my Neds:
Ryan, Austin, Carter, Shannon,
Michael, Paul Jr., and Katherine.
What an Amazing Adventure!

CHAPTER ONE

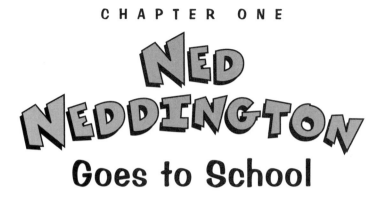

Goes to School

The first kid I met on the first day of school, in first grade, was a kid named Ned Neddington.

Ned Neddington is the smartest kid in the first grade. He told me

so on the first day of school
in first grade.

Ned Neddington wears eye glasses.
They make him look like the
smartest kid in first grade. Ned says
he has already read *Harry Potter.*
I think his eye glasses helped him
read it. I can read the *Biscuit* book.
I told my mom to get me some eye
glasses so I can read *Harry Potter*
instead of *Biscuit.*

Ned Neddington dresses like the
smartest kid in first grade. He
always buttons the top button on

his polo shirt. Sometimes I wear t-shirts, so I can't button the top button. Ned Neddington says that if you want to be smart, you must look smart. I believe him because he is the smartest kid in first grade. I unbutton my top button on the playground, except when I wear t-shirts. The kids on the playground won't pick you for teams if you button the top button on your polo shirt.

Ned Neddington wears lace-up shoes every day. He can tie his own shoes. Ned Neddington says you can't be the smartest kid in first grade if you can't tie your own shoes. I would let him tie my shoes, too, except I wear shoes, without laces. Plus, when my dad bends over to tie his lace-up shoes, he gets all red in the face and starts huffing and puffing. If I did that at school, my teacher, Ms. Thomas, would send me to the school nurse, and I might get a shot. I think I will stick with slip-ons.

Ned Neddington sits in the front row of desks right in front of our teacher. He brought Ms. Thomas an apple on the first day of school. Ned Neddington must be the smartest kid in first grade to know that Ms. Thomas likes apples. One problem with Ned's choice of seats is that he is a sitting duck for the kids in the back of class who shoot spit wads at the smartest kid in first grade.

Ned Neddington raises his hand all the time in class. He knows the answers to all the questions Ms. Thomas asks. Sometimes, Ms. Thomas ignores Ned Neddington's raised hand and calls on other people. I just hope he isn't raising his hand to go to the bathroom.

Ned Neddington eats all the right foods in the lunchroom. He eats carrot sticks, celery sticks, yogurt, and fruit cups. He only drinks water. Ned Neddington gives me a guilty look as I gob grape jelly on white bread slices to make my famous jelly sandwich. He scolds me and says, "Don't you realize that the caloric content combined with the transfats, polyunsaturated fats, and high density lipid cholesterol content in your food could cause you to have a sudden heart attack?"

I don't understand anything Ned Neddington said about my grape jelly sandwich, but I know that if my sandwich had all that stuff in it and could do all those things, it sure must taste great. So, I made myself another one. Yum! Double down on grape jelly sandwiches. I am serious as a heart attack about that.

Ned Neddington is always at the front of the carpool line to go home. He has to get home so he can do his homework. I am sure Ned Neddington will have a healthy snack when he gets home. I'll bet he'll have raisins or something. Yuck!

Ned Neddington says he doesn't have a dog. He says a dog might eat his homework. I figure the smartest kid in first grade would feed his dog healthier food than homework paper. I hate homework. I bet if I tried to feed homework paper to my dog, Higgins, he'd hate it too.

I wave to Ned Neddington as he drives off with his nanny in a minivan, but I am already day-dreaming about the Oreos and milk waiting on me at home.

A six-year-old needs all the brain food he can get.

Ned Neddington, the smartest kid in first grade, is my first good friend at my new school. I figure being best friends with the smartest kid in first grade must have its advantages. Maybe I'll learn lots of stuff by just staying close by. I wonder why Ned Neddington would want to hang out with me for the next twelve years.

Well, Ned Neddington says that I got picked early for playground teams and the two cutest girls in first grade sat with me at lunch on the first day of school. (I knew them from kindergarten.) Ned Neddington says he is not the smartest kid in first grade for nothing. He says maybe I can use a wingman!

That night, after finishing my ice cream, brushing my teeth and hugging my dog, Higgins, I fell fast asleep dreaming about the second day of school.

THE END

CHAPTER TWO

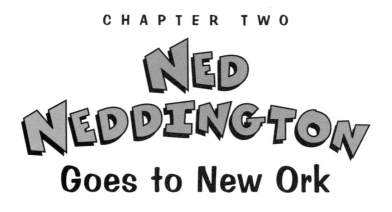

Ned Neddington
Goes to New Ork

Ned Neddington, the first kid I met on the first day of first grade, is the first kid I know who has been to New Ork. (I know it is really New York, but I say New Ork because I am only six.)

Ned Neddington knows everything about New Ork because he is the smartest kid in first grade.

Ned Neddington went to New Ork with his mom and dad. My mom and dad go to New Ork every year around Christmas. My mom and dad board our dog, Higgins, and leave us with a babysitter. I wish they would let Higgins stay at home and board the babysitter. My dad tells me that one day when I am old, gray, and fat like him, I can make the rules. He also tells me that since I know everything, I should just take over General Motors now! Between us, if I was going to take over anything, it would be that Apple Company. They seem to be on to something.

Ned Neddington knows everything about New Ork. The only thing I know about New Ork is that my mom and dad tried to bring me a snow globe from New Ork. The airport people in uniforms at the metal detector would not let them bring it on the plane because it had liquid in it. I like snow globes because when you turn them upside down and shake them, it looks like snow is falling everywhere. It never snows down south where I live. I didn't know there were dangerous liquids in snow globes. I don't think a snow globe would be a very good weapon like a light saber or sword. But next time my little sister bugs me, I am going to attack her with a snow globe.

Ned Neddington says that more people live in New Ork than in any other city in the whole United States. He says that like seven million people live in New Ork.

Ned Neddington says that all of these seven million people live there, but that the whole New Ork is only six miles big. Ned says this means there are more than one million people living in each mile of New Ork. I am sure he is right because Ned Neddington is the smartest kid in first grade. I'll bet there aren't many trees or bushes in New Ork since all those people live there. I hope they don't all drive cars. What if they were all in the carpool line at school? Everyone would be tardy and get sent to the principal. The drive-thru line at McDonald's would be way long and they would run out of Happy Meal toys.

Ned Neddington says that people walk a lot in New Ork. He says everyone seems to be in a hurry. I'll bet they are! With seven million people walking around, if you don't walk fast, someone will run over you. Ned Neddington says that there are lots of taxi cabs in New Ork. He says that they honk their horns all the time, even when there is a traffic jam and people can't move. When people honk their horns at my dad, he gets mad and waves at them but doesn't use his whole hand. Ned Neddington says that happens a lot in New Ork.

Ned Neddington went to the top of the Empire State Building. He says that the Empire State Building isn't even the tallest building in New Ork. It is hard to believe they are growing buildings taller than the Empire State Building. I saw the Empire State Building in the King Kong movie. My dad says he still can't believe that the pretty woman named Ann fell for a big, hairy ape. My mom says it reminds her of when she started dating my dad.

Ned Neddington took pictures of the Statue of Liberty. Ned says that the Statue of Liberty is a symbol of freedom that was given to the United States by France. I am glad they gave us that instead of the Eiffel Tower. I am taking a French class in first grade. Ned Neddington is taking Spanish and French, but he is the smartest kid in first grade. As soon as I learn some French, I am going to write a thank you note to France for giving us the Statue of Liberty. My dad says there is a football play called the Statue of Liberty. I just don't believe that even the biggest, hugest football man could carry that statue very far, much less throw it.

Ned Neddington says that there are two baseball teams in New Ork—the Yankees and the Mets. Ned Neddington loves baseball. He says it is "The Thinking Man's Sport." Ned Neddington is the smartest kid in first grade so, we know he is a thinking man. Ned

Neddington says Yankees are people from the north. I have a cousin who lives in Boston, but he hates the Yankees. I am confused about this. Ned Neddington says that he is a Yankee because he was born in the north. He says that Yankees are smarter than Southerners. He is the smartest kid in first grade. But I don't get it. If the Yankees are so smart, why are they all moving down here? It seems like we got it right before they did. Anyway, I don't know about the other team called the Mets. I have never met a Met. Ned

Neddington says that when the Yankees play the Mets they call it the "Subway Series." Why would anyone name a baseball game after a sandwich shop? Maybe those Yankees aren't so smart after all.

Ned Neddington brought all of his stuff from New Ork for show-and-tell at school. He had postcards and a New Ork Yankees pennant. Ned Neddington brought me a snow globe from New Ork. He must have drained out all of the dangerous liquid.

Later, on the playground, Ned Neddington told me that New Ork was the fashion center of the world. Ned Neddington says that all the new styles of jeans, shoes, shirts, and dresses start in New Ork. I was shocked that Ned noticed all this fashion, as he was still wearing his top-buttoned shirt and had the waist of his pants hiked up high. I doubt that Ned started any new fashion trends in New Ork.

Ned Neddington says there are lots of fashion models and beautiful people walking around in New Ork.

Hopefully, they were walking too fast to have time to stick their tongues out at Ned like the girls do at school. Ned said that one of the most popular items was a plaid scarf made by a company named "BRRR-Berry." It is probably named that because New Ork is so cold.

I noticed that the two cutest girls in first grade were pointing at Ned and snickering. They were obviously not aware of his newfound fashion awareness. I asked Ned if he had brought the girls anything from

New Ork, maybe a BRRR-Berry scarf, jewelry, or something else. He said, "No, not even a snow globe." I shook my head in disapproval as I walked past my new fashion savvy friend, Ned Neddington, to go flirt with the girls. I realized then that rounding the smartest kid in first grade into a chick magnet was going to be a great challenge. I offered the girls an Oreo as I waved Romeo over.

THE END

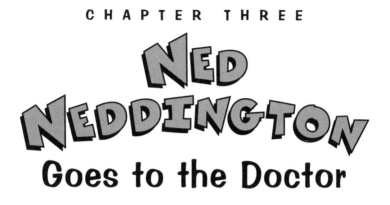

CHAPTER THREE

Goes to the Doctor

Ned Neddington, the first kid I met on the first day of first grade, went to the doctor on the first day of October. Ned Neddington said his doctor told him he bet that he was the smartest kid in the first grade. Ned Neddington's doctor must be real smart to know that.

Ned Neddington is not the first kid I have known who has gone to the doctor. I have been to the doctor lots of times too. I have a little sister and you know what that means. Every time she goes to the doctor, I have to go too. Being dragged to the doctor with your little sister when she is sick and you are well just isn't fair. Last week my little sister was sick and had to go to the doctor. Of course, my mom made me go too although I felt fine.

The shot lady, with her reading glasses pulled down low, glanced at a chart with my name on it, and said something to my mom about giving me a shot while I was there. Of all the luck! I came in well and left with a Band-Aid on my arm and a stinging pain. I sure hope we keep my sister well.

It seems like I get stuck going to the doctor with my little sister so much that I run into more friends at the doctor's office than on the playground. I even know the fish in the waiting room aquarium by

their first names. Ned Neddington
says the fish at his doctor's office
sure look good and healthy.
Ned says that means he must
have a good doctor.

Ned Neddington says that his
doctor's office has a "well" waiting
room and a "sick" waiting room.
Ned says he sat in the "well" room
so he wouldn't get sick. It would
be really bad to go to the doctor
well and end up sick. I asked Ned
Neddington why he had to go to
the doctor if he wasn't sick. Ned
Neddington said something about

"preventive medicine." He said that was the next big thing. I am going to stick with apples. If I get stuck in the "sick" room, I might sneak over to the "well" room and cough a few times. They act like snobs over there in the "well" room. Mom and Dad say at their doctor there is only one room. I guess everyone leaves there sick.

Ned Neddington says that he and his mom had to answer a bunch of questions on a piece of paper before he saw the doctor. Ned says he thinks he scored a 100. He isn't the smartest kid in the first grade for nothing. Ned Neddington says he is in the top 50th percentile in height and weight on the doctor's growth chart. I warned him that he is just a carrot stick or two away from the bottom half. The only growth chart that matters to me is the little fake man with the yard stick standing next to the roller coaster at the amusement park. When I can ride the roller coaster, I am 100%. Ned Neddington says the doctor uses a growth curve. Why is it called a curve when my mom wants me to grow up straight?

Ned Neddington says that the doctor patted him on the back for his good eating habits. Ned told the doctor that he only eats vegetables, yogurt, and fruit, and that he only drinks water. I think this might be why Ned is so close to the bottom half of the weight chart. Ned says that his doctor said my grape jelly sandwiches sound terribly unhealthy. He also told Ned "good job" for avoiding video games. My advice for Ned Neddington is that if he wants to gain weight and have more fun, he needs to change doctors.

Ned Neddington says that his doctor had to be the smartest kid back when he was in first grade. Ned says his doctor buttons the top button on his shirt and wears eye glasses. Next thing you know, Ned Neddington will show up at school in a white coat with his name on it. Ned Neddington says the doctor made him stick out his tongue and say "aah." I am sure Ned knew how to do that because the girls in first grade stick their tongues out at Ned a lot. Ned Neddington says the doctor looked in his ears with a metal gadget. The doctor's view was probably blocked by Ned's brains.

Ned Neddington says the last thing he had to do before leaving the doctor's office was to go see the shot lady. I believe every doctor has a shot lady who gives little kids shots on the way out. The shot lady's office is always next to the bulletin board with all of the Christmas cards on it. All of the kids are smiling and happy on the Christmas cards. They ought to take some pictures after kids see the shot lady.

Ned Neddington says that he waved goodbye to the fish in the "well" room on his way out. He says they cheered him up after the shot lady put a Band-Aid on his leg. Ned Neddington says he noticed that the plants in his doctor's office looked like they needed watering. I hesitated to offer advice to the smartest kid in first grade, but I told him it was a bad sign that his doctor couldn't keep his office plants alive. The smartest kid in first grade asked me for my doctor's name.

THE END

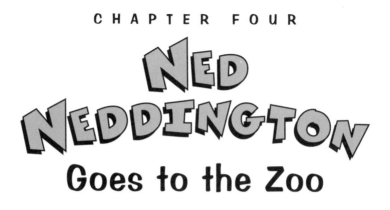

CHAPTER FOUR

Goes to the Zoo

Ned Neddington, the first kid I met on the first day of first grade, is the first kid I know to see the first baby panda, Mei Lan. Ned Neddington saw the baby panda, Mei Lan, last week when he went to the zoo.

I was surprised that the smartest kid in first grade would take time away from homework and tutors to go to the zoo. Ned called it a field trip. My dad calls it a field trip when we ride to Dunkin' Donuts or Krispy Kreme. Anyway, Ned says it is okay to go to the zoo because it is an "educational experience." He probably took notes at the zoo.

Ned Neddington says that panda bears come all the way across the ocean from a place called China. Ned Neddington says China has a thing called the Great Wall. He says the Great Wall of China is four miles long and 25 feet high. Man, and I think I have a big swing set. I wonder how those little panda bears can climb over that big wall? Maybe that tall Chinese basketball man gave them a boost.

Ned Neddington says he saw all kinds of animals at the zoo. I hope he didn't scare any of them with all of his cameras and video recorders, or by staring at them for too long. Those animals probably thought they had met that James Bond guy. But, to tell you the truth, Ned

Neddington looks more like
Harry Potter.

Ned Neddington says they also
had polar bears at the zoo. He says
they got them from the North
Pole. I like the North Pole because
Santa Claus and Rudolph live
there. I bet the sleigh flies better
with reindeer than with polar
bears. Anyway, it would be hard for
polar bears to fly a sleigh and drink
a Coke at the same time.

Ned Neddington says he really
liked the zebras at the zoo. I have

seen the zebras at the zoo, too. They remind me of the ponies my sister and I ride on at our church carnival. Ned Neddington says he once rode a pony who had one eye and no tail. Ned said his name was "Lucky." I wonder what it would take to be named "Unlucky." Ned says Lucky went real slow. He should have offered him one of his carrot sticks. I'm sure Ned did not have a sugar cube.

When my dad watches football games he calls the referee men "zebras." They do sort of look like two-legged zebras, but zebras don't wear hats. Zebras don't have yellow flags either. My dad yells at the "referee zebras" a lot. He sometimes calls them other names, too. When he calls them other names, Mom makes him put money in a jar that she keeps.

Ned Neddington says he saw lions, tigers, and leopards at the zoo. Ned says that the lion is the "King of the Jungle." I already knew that. I watch that Lion King movie a lot. Tigers and Lions play football and baseball a lot on TV. I told Ned Neddington

there was also a Tiger who was real good at golf. Ned Neddington says golf is dumb. He says it's dumb for a person to hit a little white ball, hunt it down, and hit it again until he knocks it in a little hole. I told him he should tell that to the Tiger who plays golf. That Tiger always seems to be smiling and holding a big trophy. I think the man named Tiger is real smart to play golf.

Ned Neddington says he saw giraffes and elephants at the zoo. Ned says that giraffes have the longest neck of any mammal.

Maybe giraffes could help those baby pandas get over the Great Wall of China. Ned Neddington says that the average elephant eats five pounds of peanuts a day. Ned Neddington says he is allergic to peanuts. I am allergic to celery sticks and carrot sticks. If one of those elephants was allergic to peanuts, it sure would need lots of Kleenex.

Ned Neddington says he spent a lot of time with the monkeys at the zoo. He says he saw chimpanzees, gorillas, and orangutans.

Ned Neddington says that chimps can be trained to fly airplanes and rocket ships. I told Ned that my mom's driving was scary enough. I think I will stick to my bicycle. Ned Neddington says that one monkey turned his back to him and stuck his head between his legs and made faces at him. It sounds like how the girls on the playground treat Ned. He says one monkey was picking his nose and scratching under his arm. Having seen Ned Neddington at school, I think it could be "monkey see, monkey do."

Ned Neddington says his favorite area was the snake cage. Ned Neddington says he saw the king cobra. He says that one drop of venom from the king cobra will kill someone in seconds. I guess that is why they call him the King. When my dad talks about the King, he starts shaking his leg and dancing. I don't believe it is from venom.

Ned Neddington says he saw pythons and boa constrictors at the zoo. Ned says they feed them small white mice. That sounds about as bad as celery sticks and carrot sticks to me. Anyway, my dad says not to feel sorry for the mice. He says it is probably a better way to go than having the mice sample diet soda. I read it myself on the can that diet soda can be hazardous to laboratory animals.

Ned Neddington says he packed a healthy snack of raisins and granola bars for his trip to the zoo. When I go to the zoo, I always get my dad to buy me junk food like cotton candy, chocolate coated peanuts, and a slushy. I figure if I end up falling in the cage with the lions, tigers, and bears, I stand a better chance of making friends with them.

Ned Neddington brought me back a postcard of a gorilla from the zoo. I told him thanks. He said the two cutest girls in first grade still stuck their tongues out at him at recess. He says he didn't bring them anything from the zoo. I told Ned Neddington if monkeys could learn to fly airplanes, surely the smartest kid in first grade could figure out that stuffed animals or jewelry could win over even the coldest heart. Ned gave me a wink as he munched on a celery stick.

THE END

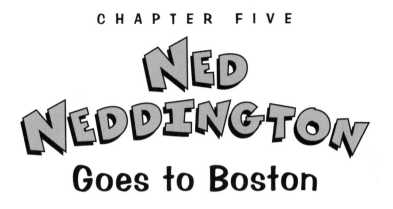

CHAPTER FIVE

Ned Neddington

Goes to Boston

Ned Neddington, the first kid I met on the first day of school in first grade, is the first kid I know who went to Boston for the World Series. Ned Neddington says at the first game in the first inning that the first Red Sock smacked a home run on the first pitch.

Ned Neddington says that the Boston Red Sox were playing the Colorado Rockies in the World Series. I know about the Red Sox because that was the name of my first tee-ball team when I was four. My Red Sox tee-ball team did not win the World Series. Our coaches said we tied every game. Ned Neddington says that tying a ball game is like "kissing your sister." Yuck! If I had had to kiss my little sister after every one of those tie tee-ball games, I believe I would just have given up and forfeited.

Ned Neddington says that Boston is famous for something called The Boston Tea Party. I know a little bit about Boston because my cousins live there. I have actually been to Boston, but I have never seen the Tea Party. Ned Neddington says that the Boston Tea Party was when a bunch of people got mad about taxes and threw all of their tea in the ocean. It seems like every spring my mom and dad fuss about taxes. Instead of throwing the tea out, my dad has to put money in the "bad word jar" because of all the things he says about a man with the initials "I.R.S."

Anyway, if those people in Boston had thrown their tea in the ocean, the tea would be really salty. Maybe that's why they don't have sweet tea in Boston. The only tea party I have ever seen is my little sister and her annoying friends having a tea party. I wish I could find a harbor to throw them in.

Ned Neddington says that the Boston Red Sox are his favorite baseball team. My dad says Ned may be riding a "bandwagon." I have a red wagon. It would not hold a band. I can't figure out why anyone would name a baseball team after a pair of socks. Socks must be a good name for a baseball team since there is a team called the White Sox who play in Chicago. My mom says that our washer and dryer at home have a sock monster. She says that the sock monster makes our socks disappear all the time. It would be really bad if the Red Sox and White

Sox had a sock monster at their house. They would have to change their names to something like Lions, Tigers, or Bears.

Ned Neddington says that at the stadium where the Red Sox play, there is a Green Monster. He says this monster is in left field and is over 37 feet tall. I have seen some green monsters on television, so I asked Ned Neddington if the Red Sox Green Monster looked like Godzilla, the Hulk, or Shrek. Ned Neddington says the Boston Green Monster looks more like a wall.

I don't think a green wall would be very scary, even if it is 37 feet tall. I am glad they do not make any movies about the Boston Green Monster wall. Those movies would be more boring than my little sister's Barbie movies.

Ned Neddington says that there are a lot of smart people in Boston. Ned Neddington says there are a lot of colleges in Boston where all these smart people go to school. He says the most famous college where smart people go in Boston is a school named Harvard. I bet they sell a lot of eye glasses to those people at Harvard so they can read lots of books. I know about Harvard because my uncle is a doctor there. He wears eye glasses, too. Harvard must be a smart college because my dad calls his school the University of Georgia, the Harvard of the South, and my dad tells me how smart that school is. Ned Neddington says there is a place called Harvard Square where smart people sit outside reading books, drinking coffee, and playing chess. I told him that when he goes to Harvard they will probably have to name it the Harvard Pentagon and add another side.

Ned Neddington says that his favorite restaurant in Boston is a place called "Legal Seafood." I wonder if this is where all the lawyers eat. I also wonder what kind of food they would serve if there was a place called "Illegal Seafood." I asked Ned Neddington if they have a health food plate at Legal Seafood. He replied that he had learned a lot from watching me in the lunchroom and decided to let his hair down when he was at

"Legal Seafood." Ned Neddington says he ordered the fried seafood platter with a "Shirley Temple." I was so impressed that I told Ned Neddington that those smart people at Harvard could probably use a smart kid like him.

Ned Neddington brought me back a t-shirt from Boston College. Ned Neddington says his dad told him that the prettiest girls went to that school. Hey, Harvard isn't for everyone. Ned Neddington brought the two cutest girls in first grade each a Red Sox key ring.

I squeezed my chair in between Ned and his two new coed lunch buddies. He winked at me as he munched on the cookies they had traded him for his raisins. The Harvard-bound, smartest kid in first grade was finally catching on.

THE END

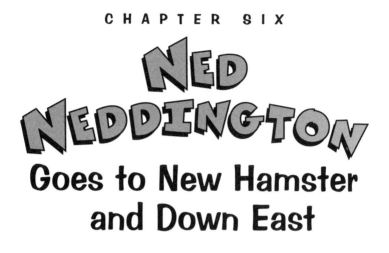

CHAPTER SIX

NED NEDDINGTON

Goes to New Hamster and Down East

Ned Neddington, the first kid I met on the first day of first grade, is the first kid I know to visit the State of New Hamster. (My dad told me it is really New Hampshire, but I am only six, so I call it New

Hamster.) Ned Neddington visited New Hamster during December on our first holiday break in first grade.

Ned Neddington and his family visited Varmant and Main, too. My mom says it is really Vermont, but Varmant sounds like a cousin of New Hamster and since I am only six, I call it Varmant. Mom and Dad also told me that Main has an "e" on the end, but I am only six and the "e" is silent anyway, so I spell it "Main." Ned Neddington says that his family started out in New Hamster, then traveled down east to Varmant and Main. He said the locals call it going down east when one travels from New Hamster to Varmant and Main. I looked at it on my globe, and it looked more like "going across" to me, but I was not going to argue with the future Geography Bowl MVP. It all just sounded cold to me anyway.

Speaking of cold, Ned Neddington says it was freezing in New Hamster. I asked Ned Neddington if there were any Disney Worlds or amusement parks in New Hamster, Varmant, or

Main. Ned gave me a look as if I had asked him if Varmant bears used indoor plumbing. Ned responded, "No, they would have to put up a dome over them to keep people warm." I guess "It's A Small World" would be even smaller in a dome. Also, that repeating song would really drive you crazy echoing in a dome.

Ned Neddington says he feels twenty pounds lighter on the playground back in Georgia. Ned says with down jackets, hoods, long johns, wool socks, and gloves on, he could barely breathe in New Hamster. I thought, gosh, if you can't breathe, that defeats the purpose of having all that clean air in New Hamster and down east.

Ned Neddington says that the first Presidential primary election is always held in New Hamster. Ned looked at me cynically and said, "You do know it is an election year, don't you?" I said, "Of course," but personally I was watching more Cartoon Network, ESPN and playing video games than watching CNN or "Meet the Press."

Ned Neddington knows the names of all the people who are running for President. I told Ned that when I do see the politicians on TV, none of them are "running." It looks to me like they are "talking" for President instead of running. Ned Neddington told me I should be more civic minded. Until Ned said that, I thought Civic was a car my babysitter drove.

Ned Neddington says they don't have taxes in New Hamster. If it weren't so cold in New Hamster, I bet a bunch of people would move there. I don't know anything about taxes except my mom and dad get grumpy every April. I wonder if New Hamster had a Tea Party like they did in Boston to get rid of taxes. But I don't think New Hamster has an ocean to throw the tea in.

I asked Ned Neddington if there was an Old Hamster before there was a New Hamster. He just shook his head at me and mumbled something about cousins getting married.

Ned Neddington says that they only spent one day in the State of Varmant. Ned said in the state capital of Varmant, a city called Montpelier, there is not one single McDonald's. Heck, with no McDonald's, one day would be way too long for me.

Ned Neddington explained that Varmant is famous for maple syrup. I thought this was certainly refreshing news on the heels of the anti-McDonald's state capital, but I didn't think maple syrup would do Ned much good with his celery sticks and fruit cups. Every morning with my pancakes, I pour on some Varmant syrup, thank Varmant for this treat, and pray they get a McDonald's.

My dad says that Ben and Jerry's ice cream is made in Varmant. That makes sense. The cows that make the milk for Ben and Jerry's ice cream are probably so cold outside in Varmant that it is easy for them to make ice cream.

I am a little confused about Varmant. How can a state that has cows make Ben and Jerry's ice cream and yummy maple syrup have a capital city without a McDonald's. That is like a Happy Meal with no toy prize.

Ned Neddington says he really liked the State of Main. I was a little confused on why New Hamster should have the first "primary" if there was a state named "Main." I will figure that out as I become more civic minded.

Ned Neddington says there is a humongous store in Main called

L.L. Bean. He says the L.L. Bean store is almost as big as the whole state of Varmant. Maybe there are a few McDonald's inside L.L. Bean.

Ned Neddington says that L.L. Bean sells all kinds of outdoor clothes. It sounds like they need them in Main, Varmant and New Hamster. Ned says that Mr. L.L. Bean started his company many years back when he invented the Maine Hunting Shoe. With a name like Bean, I figured L.L. would be a farmer and not a hunter. I guess he could be both. Just think how big the store would be if that man who invented Crocs builds one.

I asked Ned if the Maine Hunting Shoe went on the left foot or the right foot. He gave me another one of those looks. I believe my dad has some L.L. Bean shoes. He puts them on when he forgets to shave and carries in firewood.

Ned Neddington said that his favorite city in Main was a place named Bath. How could anyone name a city after an activity like taking a bath? I wonder if Main has cities named "Shower," "Scrub," or "Brush." If my parents moved me to a city named "Bath," I would run away to that city with no McDonald's. Yuck! I hate the bathtub and I bet I would hate that Bath city too!

Ned Neddington says that Main produces most of the lobsters caught in the United States. Ned Neddington says that the lobster men catch the lobsters in traps they set out in the water. How do they get the lobsters red for the Red Lobster restaurants?

Ned Neddington says that it is illegal in Main to catch a lobster with your bare hands. Have you seen the huge pinchers on those lobsters? I figure the smartest kid in first grade would know better than trying to grab a lobster barehanded. In my opinion, the people making laws in Main should spend more time naming cities and less time on barehanded lobster catching.

At the first show and tell at school after the holiday break, Ned Neddington showed the class

political bumper stickers from New Hamster, maple syrup from Varmant, and an L.L. Bean t-shirt from Main. I brought back trinkets from Disney World. I also brought back a good suntan from the Sunshine State.

I noticed that the two cutest girls in first grade had invited Ned Neddington over to the monkey bars at recess. I looked at him with a wry smile and put my hands out as if to ask, "What's your secret?" I noticed that both girls had teddy bears from Varmant and Ben &

Jerry's gift certificates in their book bags. I marveled at the great strides Casanova made in four short months as my wingman. Ned Neddington gave me a high five as he unbuttoned his polo.

THE END

CHAPTER SEVEN

Ned Neddington
Goes on Spring Break

Ned Neddington, the first kid I met on the first day of first grade, is the first kid I know to go snow skiing during our spring break in first grade. Ned and his family went snow skiing out west in Colorado.

Ned Neddington is the smartest kid in first grade. He told me so on the first day of school in first grade. He has reminded me everyday since school started.

Spring break is the break we get from school between winter and spring. I wonder why the smartest kid in first grade would want to go play in the snow as we are welcoming spring. I guess snow skiing must make kids smarter.

I was right. Ned Neddington says that when you go snow skiing, your parents put you in ski school. I knew there must have been something educational about Ned's spring break.

Ned Neddington says he was excited when he heard there would be ski school on his snow skiing trip. He didn't want to take a week off and slip from being number one to number two. Ned Neddington calls being number two in class the same as being "first-last." I think number two means something else that is also bad.

Ned Neddington says that ski school is different from real school. He says at ski school the teachers taught him how to ski, and not how to be smarter. I think that sounded fun. Anyway, Ned can't get much smarter.

Ned Neddington says that to snow ski you have to wear uncomfortable boots. I don't think regular boots would go very fast in the snow. Ned explained that the boots snap onto skis, and the skis cause you to go fast down a hill. Ned says he crashed into several other kids in ski school and caused a big log pile in the snow. He probably had his hand up trying to answer all the ski school teacher's questions.

Ned Neddington says that he had to wear a helmet while he was snow skiing. I said, "Darn, Ned. You weren't playing football or riding a motorcycle." The helmet was probably to protect the trees from Ned's hard head. I bet he needed an extra large helmet to cover all his brains.

Ned Neddington says that the first thing they teach you in ski school is how to stop when skiing downhill. He says the teachers call it "doing the pizza." It's when you point your skis inward and make a triangle. I think they should have used some other health food example for putting on the brakes to explain it to Ned. Something like triangles of celery sticks, carrot sticks, or fruit wedges would be better. Ned Neddington has never eaten pizza so he probably had a hard time "doing the pizza."

Ned Neddington says that once he learned how to stop, the ski teachers let him go up the mountain. Ned says that he rode a chair lift way high up the mountain. Ned Neddington says there is a bar on the front of the chair lift to keep you from falling out. Ned says that one time he forgot to lift the bar and he had to stay on the chair and ride it back down again. The other skiers were probably glad. At least on the chair lift, Ned couldn't wipe them out as he tried to stop using his carrot stick or fruit wedge technique.

Ned Neddington says there are trail maps the skiers use to know where they should ski and to help them avoid getting lost. I figure that Ned Neddington probably read the trail maps at night for fun. Ned was probably reading the trail map when he forgot to raise the bar on the chair lift.

Ned Neddington says that after skiing each day, he and his family would get in the hot tub. I know about hot tubs because my dad calls it an Alabama hot tub when I pass gas in the bath tub. I also know a lot about being in hot water. My parents say I am in hot water when I get written up for talking too much at school and when I pick on my annoying little sister.

Ned Neddington says the Colorado hot tub was actually outside. Ned says the water was very hot in the Colorado hot tub even though it was freezing outside. Ned says they would wear nothing but their swimsuits outside in the freezing weather in the hot Colorado hot tub. It all seemed very confusing to me: folks being half-naked in freezing weather sitting in hot water. But it did sound nicer than my Alabama hot tub.

Ned Neddington says that the people who live out in Colorado and ski a lot are called "locals." Ned says that the locals didn't read the trail maps nearly as much as he did. Ned says the locals talk funny. Ned says the locals called everyone "dude." Ned says the locals started lots of sentences with the phrase "Like it was real awesome, dude." Ned says the locals use the word "richter" (as in Richter Scale), to describe something hugely cool, as in, "That air I just got was like really richter, dude."

I told Ned Neddington not to try talking like the locals back on the playground at school. I just couldn't see Ned Neddington calling the kids on the playground "dude" or describing a great football play as "like richter, dude." Hey, I made real progress with Ned on the playground in eight months and he didn't need a peer group sacking now. I mean, he was unbuttoning his top button, high-fiving people, and putting down the latest Harry Potter book these days. Ned Neddington had even been picked early for playground teams. Okay, I was usually captain and I had to look after my wingman. But I knew that Ned Neddington was just a misplaced "dude" or "richter" from being banished back to learned spectator.

Ned Neddington says that while out west his family took a day off from skiing and went snowmobiling. Ned says they rode snowmobiles to a place called The Continental Divide.

Ned Neddington says The Continental Divide is the place on the North American continent where the water decides which way it will flow. Ned Neddington says that all the water east of the Continental Divide flows to the Atlantic Ocean and all the water to the west of the Continental Divide flows to the Pacific Ocean. All this time I just thought that water flowed downhill.

Anyway, the Continental Divide sounded like a math problem for Ned Neddington to solve, as he was already doing division in math at school. I bet Ned Neddington figured out an equation to solve the Continental Divide before his snowmobile made it back that day.

Ned Neddington brought trail maps back from the ski slopes to show our class on share day. Ned had the trail maps memorized. Ned Neddington brought me back a snow globe from Colorado. He said he packed it in his checked luggage so all the dangerous liquid would stay in the snow globe. I am happy to have another weapon in my arsenal for my continuing battles with my annoying little sister. I find that in fighting with your little sister, you can never have enough light sabers, swords, or snow globes.

As the two cutest girls in first grade made their way to sit with us at lunch, I could tell they were expecting a nice souvenir from Ned Neddington's trip out west. I quickly whispered to Ned, "Well what did you bring the chicks?" He replied, "Dude, I think the chicks have gotten a little spoiled."

Ned asked, "Have you heard the expression, 'Like, they are high maintenance?'" Ned said, "Gotta keep 'em grounded and guessing." I barely had time to say "Dude you rock, like, that is so richter" before the two cutest girls in first grade sat down next to us.

Nothing like a little souvenir let down to keep the girls in their place. Leave it to the smartest kid in first grade to unravel the mystery of the opposite sex. "Dude!"

THE END

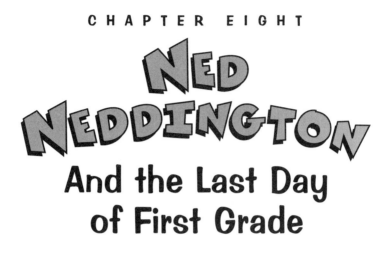

CHAPTER EIGHT

And the Last Day
of First Grade

Ned Neddington, the first kid I
met on the first day of first grade,
is the first kid I saw on the last day
of school in first grade.

Ned Neddington was the smartest

kid in first grade on the first day of school in first grade and he is still the smartest kid in first grade on the last day of school. Ned Neddington told me he was still the smartest kid in the first grade on the last day of school.

The first thing they do on the last day of school in first grade is hold an awards ceremony. The parents of all the first grade students come to the awards ceremony. Parents also bring our annoying little brothers and sisters.

The awards ceremony for first grade students is held on the last day of school in the school auditorium. Ned Neddington proved he was the smartest kid in first grade at the awards ceremony. Ned received all of the awards for real school stuff. Ned Neddington won the award for best reader, best speller, best math student, and the award as the best overall student in first grade. We all call that the "teacher's pet" award. I really thought he should have received the "Johnny Appleseed award" for all the apples he brought Ms. Thomas throughout first grade.

Speaking of apples, I tricked Ned Neddington once when I asked him if when eating an apple he would rather find a whole worm or half of a worm. I actually had to explain to the smartest kid in first grade why you would rather find an intact worm rather than what was left of the half you had eaten.

Anyway, Ned Neddington racked up so many awards at the awards ceremony that it was almost embarrassing. At one point, I heard several parents muttering "This is like "George Strait,"

"Alabama," or "Titanic." (My mom and dad told me that these are people, groups or movies that have won lots of awards.) I have seen the Titanic movie once but I got sort of bored because I knew the boat was going to sink. At least, since the boat sank, there won't be any Titanic II or Titanic III like Shrek.

I received the award for "most athletic" in first grade. I noticed that the two cutest girls in first grade were clapping loudly for me as I walked past them to the stage to receive my certificate from Ms. Thomas. I think my parents were just glad that I had successfully finished first grade. I heard my dad whisper previously that I had been "held back in sandbox."

As I returned to my seat next to Ned Neddington, Ned remarked, "Congratulations. Someone else needed to win an award besides me. Perhaps your athletic skills will compensate for your academic shortcomings." I wasn't exactly sure what Ned Neddington meant, but I am certain it was sarcastic and not flattering.

It didn't bother me since most of the college football players I saw on the television listed their college majors as "undecided" or "undergraduate studies." I was confident I could excel in the "undecided" major in college. My dad says that my older brothers who are in college are doing well in their double majors of girls and party. Heck, that sounds even better than undecided. I might change my major.

After the awards ceremony, the first grade class went outside for the traditional year ending "Olympic Field Day" events. The field day events held much more promise for me than the academic awards. Unfortunately, Ned Neddington did not rack up any awards during field day. Frankly, I was just glad that my wingman survived field day. Ned Neddington made a mess of himself in the egg toss as he was a little too aggressive, catching the egg instead of cradling it. Ned almost amputated the leg of one of our classmates during the three-legged race.

The worst by far, however, was Ned Neddington's allergic reaction meltdown during the sack race. It seems that poor Ned is wildly allergic to the burlap bag, causing him to cough and sneeze through an entire box of Kleenex. The teachers were only about two Kleenex away from calling the school nurse when Ned's sneezing fit ended and order was restored to the field day. Ned's parents had listed all of his allergies including eggs, peanut butter, flour, latex, and gluten (whatever that is) with Ms. Thomas but had apparently omitted burlap sacks. My dad, the lawyer, says that Ned's allergic attack from the sack will probably be the death of the field day sack race. He said something about Ned having a new name—Plaintiff.

After the field day and prior to dismissing all of the first grade students on the last day, we all signed each other's yearbooks. I read in many yearbooks how Ned had begun his statement with dude.

Calling his classmates dude did not quite fit with Ned's other statements in the notes such as "Dude, I have enjoyed this ethereal, eclectic first grade experience with you." As I signed Ned Neddington's yearbook I noticed where many of our classmates called Ned names such as "Nerdly," "Snedly," "Ned Ned," and even "Needleton." I simply wrote, "Dear Ned, thanks for being my first good friend in first grade. Thanks for all the help with my homework. I have enjoyed having you as a wingman."

I read with interest Ned Neddington's entry in my yearbook. He wrote, "Dude, thanks for hanging out with me this year. Work hard on your cursive and concentrate on your multiplication tables. Turn your baseball cap around. I hope to see you over the summer. Ned Neddington."

I was drinking a cup of punch and munching on a slice of pizza while chatting with the two cutest girls in first grade at the dismissal party prior to the end of the last day of first grade. Ned Neddington walked up with a Kleenex in his hands, wiping his eyes and nose from the burlap sack allergy attack. He was clutching a plastic baggy full of celery sticks and carrot sticks. Ned Neddington pulled a sheet of paper from his back pocket and asked "Have you all seen the summer reading list for the second grade? I have already read half of the books and will finish the other half in a few weeks." My mind was racing with the excitement of the upcoming summer. I was thinking more of hanging out at the swimming pool, playing baseball, going on vacation and maybe summer camp. I told Ned Neddington to give the reading list a rest as I handed him a cookie. Minutes later I noticed that the two cutest girls in first grade had cornered Ned Neddington and they each had their arms around him.

As I waited in carpool line with Ned Neddington I asked him how he had charmed the girls at the party. Ned Neddington replied, "Dude, you have to work every angle. Ghost writing a few book reports is a lot cheaper than buying

souvenirs." I almost asked Ned Neddington if he could use a wingman before he stepped into his mom's minivan and drove away.

The weathermen were calling for a long, hot summer. I couldn't wait to get it started.

THE END

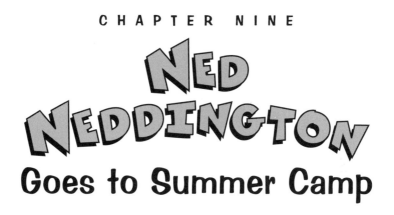

CHAPTER NINE

Goes to Summer Camp

Ned Neddington is the first kid I know who went to summer camp after our first grade year. Ned Neddington went to summer camp in North Georgia where he lived in a cabin with other kids for a week.

Ned's cabin mates probably all came home smarter. I keep thinking he will rub off on me. My parents hope he will too.

Ned Neddington said he had a great time at summer camp. Ned says there were some things that annoyed him about camp. Ned says he had to make up his bed every day.

Ned says he could have stayed home and done that. I agree with Ned about that. Making up my bed is a pet peeve of mine. Why should I make up my bed once it is good and comfortable and broken in when I have to get back in the same bed that same night? At least I have a twin bed. My annoying little sister has to make up her queen size bed every day.

Anyway, Ned Neddington says that the camp counselors would grade his bed every day to see how well he did in making it up. Ned says they would drop a quarter on his bed to see how high it would bounce. The higher the quarter bounced, the better. It meant the bed was made up good and tight.

I'm surprised Ned Neddington didn't sneak some experimental spring like material under his covers to add bounce to his bed. Ned Neddington says he received a "B" on his bed make up grade. He is probably permanently scarred because of this. I'm sure Ned plans an appeal.

Ned Neddington didn't like the shower situation at summer camp. For one thing, Ned says he thought going to summer camp would get him out of bathing at all for a week.

Ned Neddington says he had to wear flip-flops in the shower for fear of getting athlete's feet. Well, now, I have seen Ned play sports on the playground. Frankly, I think he is in desperate need of developing athlete's feet, athlete's hands, athlete's arms, and athlete's body for that matter. If he could catch athlete's feet in the shower, then I think Ned should ditch the flip-flops. Then again, if there is anyone who might be immune to athlete's feet it would be Ned. Either way, he didn't need flip-flops.

Ned Neddington says the campers ate their meals in a place called the mess hall. Now that is a name I can relate to. It sounds more like my room than a dining hall. I think I will ask my mom if we can rename my bedroom "The Mess Hall."

Ned Neddington didn't like the food served in the mess hall. Ned says mess is an appropriate name for the food. Ned says he didn't have to worry about the food because his parents ordered a special diet for him.

Ned says he ate his usual staple of yogurt, celery sticks, carrot sticks, fruit cups, and water. I'll bet the other campers prefer the mess in the mess hall over Ned Neddington's health food mess.

I am going to find a summer camp with McDonald's or Chick-fil-A. Who wants to go to a summer camp without chicken fingers? By the way, if chickens don't have hands, where do they get chicken fingers? And you know what else? Buffaloes don't have wings either. I guess all I care about is that every restaurant in America has chicken fingers and buffalo wings. Is this a great country or what?

Ned Neddington says in his summer camp all of the campers swam in a large lake. Ned said he had only swam in a swimming pool prior to summer camp. I didn't think Ned should have any problem swimming in a lake since the girls at school were always telling Ned to go jump in a lake.

Ned Neddington says that the camp counselors took him and the other campers on a snipe hunt. Ned says that a snipe is a bird that can't fly. Ned says that you hunt for snipe at night. Several of the campers would carry sacks to catch the snipe in. The other campers would use sticks to scare the snipe into the sacks to be captured. Ned says he was one of the sack holders. Ned says that he hunted the snipe birds for several hours but he never saw any snipe birds.

Ned Neddington says that he thinks the snipe bird should be added to the national endangered species list.

Ned says he intends to write his Congressman a letter about the rare snipe bird. My dad says the snipe bird has been rare since he was a kid. He told me to tell Ned not to worry about the rare snipe bird.

I met Ned Neddington at the neighborhood swimming pool late in the summer just before the start of second grade. The two cutest girls from first grade were together at the pool. Ned Neddington tried to impress them with a dive he learned at camp, but his flip turned into a belly flop and splashed the girls. I

covered for him and blamed the bad dive on a slip as I charged a round of snow cones to my parents' account.

My friendship with Ned Neddington, the smartest kid in first grade, held such great promise. I was daydreaming about his help with a book report here or a science project there in exchange for the small price of helping shape this brilliantly nerdy kid into "rock star" cool.

Just then, the two cutest girls in first grade hand-splashed me in the face with water and asked me if

Ned and I would like to come over for an end of summer cookout at their house. I knew this was no snipe hunt. I said yes, as I threw Ned a towel.

Ned Neddington could take one night off from his head start on the second grade summer reading list. I could procrastinate and not start the reading list for one more night as well. Second grade, although inevitably fabulous, would have to take a backseat to a late August night's cookout.

THE END

Paul Weathington was born in Carrollton, Georgia.
He is an Atlanta attorney who has written over 20
children's books. Mr. Weathington derives much of his
material from his experiences with his seven children.
He formed JuneKat Books, LLC in 2007. His other works
may be seen and previewed at www.JuneKatBooks.com

Other books by Paul Weathington

Bed Bugs Don't Bite is based on the time-honored bedtime expression parents and grandparents utter when tucking the kids in. In the book, children sneak a flashlight under the covers and explore the "undercover world of the Bed Bugs." They find ladybugs, caterpillars, bumble bees, ants, and butterflies, and learn that the bugs would rather party all night than bite. Fully illustrated, for ages 2 to 8.

Counting Sheep Doesn't Make Me Sleep is a rhythming tale about a child's attempt to go to sleep by counting sheep. He sees all his favorite, wonderful things and has a great night's sleep—there's just one problem—he never sees any sheep. It seems the old "counting sheep" suggestion is a parental trick. An excellent bedtime book, and also good for young readers. Fully illustrated, for ages 2 to 8.

Where is the Man On the Moon? involves a young girl's attempt to spot the man who lives on the moon. Is the man really on the moon rock, or is this just parental crock? This book has eye-catching illustrations of outer space, astronauts and even subtle adult music themes. Great bedtime book, and also good for early readers.

Ish, Ish, Almost Made a Fish explores our use of the "ish" phrase and ponders where we would be if Ish had become a Fish, a Wish or a Dish, instead of just little ole non-fish Ish. Great fun! Fully illustrated with watercolors. Great book to read to children at bedtime, and also an excellent early reader book.

Lightning Shoes is an inspirational soccer book which illustrates the powerful impact of coaches' motivational words. It packs a powerful parental message as well. The book is both a good bedtime story and an excellent book for early readers. Fully illustrated, for ages 2 to 10.